KU-350-748

ALLIGATOR TAILS
and CROCODILE CAKES

NICOLA MOON

Illustrated by
ANDY ELLIS

KING*fisher*

For my parents – N.M.
To Hayley – A.E.

KINGFISHER

An imprint of Kingfisher Publications Plc
New Penderel House, 283-288 High Holborn
London WC1V 7HZ

First published by Kingfisher 1996
6 8 10 9 7
6TR/1000/TWP/PR(FR)/150AM

Text copyright © Nicola Moon 1996
Illustrations copyright © Andy Ellis 1996

Educational Adviser: Prue Goodwin
Reading and Language Centre
University of Reading

All rights reserved. No part of this publication
may be reproduced, stored in a retrieval system or
transmitted by any means electronic, mechanical,
photocopying or otherwise, without the prior
permission of the publisher.

A CIP catalogue record for this book
is available from the British Library.

ISBN 1 85697 335 2

Printed in Singapore

Contents

Hide and Seek

Crocodile was playing hide and seek

with his friend Alligator.

Crocodile closed his eyes

and started counting.

"One, two, three, four, five, six..."

Alligator looked for somewhere to hide.

He found a big tree.

He stood behind the tree

and pulled himself up

as tall as he could.

"Coming, ready or not," called Crocodile.

He looked to the left.

He looked to the right.

He looked up and he looked down.

And then...

"Found you! Found you!

I can see your tail!" he sang.

"I want to hide again," said Alligator.

"And this time you won't find me."

So Crocodile closed his eyes

and started counting.

"One, two, three, four, five, six, seven..."

Alligator looked for somewhere to hide.

He found a space between two rocks.

He squeezed himself in

and made himself as thin as he could.

"Coming, ready or not!" called Crocodile.

He looked to the left.

He looked to the right.

He looked up and he looked down.

And then...

"Found you! Found you!

I can see your tail!" he sang.

"I want to hide again," said Alligator.

"And this time you really won't find me."

So Crocodile closed his eyes

and started counting.

"One, two, three, four,

five, six, seven, eight..."

Alligator looked for somewhere to hide.

He found a hedge.

He wriggled under the hedge

and made himself as flat as he could.

"Coming, ready or not!" called Crocodile.

He looked to the left.

He looked to the right.

He looked up and he looked down.

And then...

"Found you! Found you!

I can see your tail!" he sang.

"I want to hide again," said Alligator.
"And this time you really, definitely
won't find me."
So Crocodile closed his eyes
and started counting.
"One, two, three, four,
five, six, seven, eight, nine..."

Alligator looked for somewhere to hide.

He found an old barrel.

He climbed in and curled up.

He made himself as small as he could.

"Coming, ready or not!" called Crocodile.

He looked to the left.

He looked to the right.

He looked up and he looked down.

And then...

"Found you! Found you!

I can see your tail!" he sang.

"I want to hide again," said Alligator.
"And this time you really, definitely,
positively won't be able to find me.
NO WAY!"
So Crocodile closed his eyes
and started counting.

"One, two, three, four,
five, six, seven, eight, nine, ten..."

This time Alligator didn't look
for somewhere to hide.
He crept up close behind Crocodile
and kept as still and quiet as he could.

"Coming, ready or not!" called Crocodile.

He looked to the left.

He looked to the right.

He looked up

and he looked down.

But he didn't look behind him.

"BOO!" shouted Alligator.

"I knew you wouldn't find me!"

"My turn to hide now," said Crocodile.

"Mind you don't leave your tail

sticking out," said Alligator.

Crocodile and Alligator
Bake a Cake

Crocodile and Alligator were baking a cake.
Crocodile had his grandma's recipe book
and an enormous mixing bowl.

Alligator was opening all the cupboards.

"We need some flour," said Crocodile.

"What's flour?" said Alligator.

"It's white and soft and dusty,"
said Crocodile.

"And it's in a blue bag."
As he spoke, a blue bag
wobbled
and toppled
and landed POOF!
on the floor
at Alligator's feet.

"Like this?" asked Alligator.

"Yes," said Crocodile. "That's flour."

Crocodile put four big spoonfuls

of flour into the bowl.

Alligator swept up the mess.

"We need some eggs," said Crocodile.

"How many?" asked Alligator.

"Two," said Crocodile. "Two large eggs."

Alligator picked two big brown eggs

out of the basket.

"I saw someone juggle with eggs once,"

he said. "Like this..."

SPLAT! SPLOSH!

Alligator wasn't very good at juggling.

Luckily there were two more eggs left.
Crocodile cracked the eggs
against the side of the bowl,
opened the shells,
and let the eggs
drop onto
the flour.

"You must be more careful, Alligator."
"I will," said Alligator,
cleaning up the mess.

"We need some margarine," said Crocodile.

"Where will I find that?" asked Alligator.

"In the fridge," said Crocodile.

"In a large white tub."

Alligator opened the fridge

and took out the large white tub.

He tried to open the lid.

It was very tight.

"Can you open it for me, please?"

Crocodile pulled
and tugged
and heaved
and...PLOP!

The lid shot off
and Crocodile
dropped the tub
onto the floor.
Upside down.

31

"You must be more careful, Crocodile,"
laughed Alligator.

"Don't be cheeky," said Crocodile,
and he picked up the tub.

Luckily there was still some margarine left.

Alligator wiped up the mess.

"We need some sugar," said Crocodile.

"I know where the sugar is," said Alligator.

"I like sugar."

He reached up and carefully lifted down
the jar marked SUGAR.

"Mind you don't slip..."

said Crocodile.

CRASH!

It was too late.

Alligator sat on the floor

looking miserable,

covered in sticky sugar.

"I don't think I'm very good

at making cakes," he said.

"You just need to be more careful,"

said Crocodile.

He weighed out

what was left of the sugar.

Alligator looked sadly at the mess.

"All we need now are some raisins,"

said Crocodile.

"You can weigh them if you like,"

he added.

Alligator cheered up.

He weighed the raisins

and put them into a little dish.

"We add them later," explained Crocodile.

"May I taste one?" asked Alligator.

"Just one," said Crocodile,

who was busy plugging in the electric mixer.

Alligator ate a raisin.

Then another one.

And another...

Then just one more.

"We're ready for the mixing,"
said Crocodile.
"Stand back!"

Crocodile switched on the mixer.

WHOOSH!

The flour and eggs
and margarine and sugar
spun round in the bowl so fast
it made Alligator dizzy.

"Is that really going to turn into a cake?"

asked Alligator,

looking at the creamy mixture.

"A delicious cake," said Crocodile.

He switched off the mixer.

"Now it's time for you

to stir in the raisins."

Crocodile poured
the mixture
into a big round tin
and put it into the oven to bake.
"Now we can clean up the mess," he said.
"And when we've finished
the cake will be ready."

They mopped

and swept

and wiped

and polished the floor.

Crocodile washed

the mixing bowl and the spoon

and cleaned the mixer.

"Mmmm!" said Alligator.

"I smell something good."

"I think the cake is ready,"

said Crocodile.

He lifted it out of the oven very carefully.

When the cake was cool,

Crocodile cut two huge slices,

and poured out two glasses of lemonade.

"Scrumptious!" said Alligator.

"I'm good at *eating* cakes!"

"There don't seem to be many raisins in it,"
said Crocodile.

45

"May I have another piece?"

asked Alligator.

"Only if you sweep up the crumbs,"

said Crocodile.

"Just look at the mess you're making!"

About the Author and Illustrator

Nicola Moon began writing books for children four years ago. Before that she was a teacher. Nicola says, "When I was a child hide and seek was one of my favourite games. I can remember helping to make cakes too, just like Alligator."

Andy Ellis has written and illustrated lots of children's books. He also works on film animations for television. "Trying to make an alligator and a crocodile look friendly wasn't easy, but I hope the readers will think I've succeeded!"

If you've enjoyed reading
Alligator Tails and Crocodile Cakes
try these other **I Am Reading** books:

BARN PARTY
Claire O'Brien & Tim Archbold

GRANDAD'S DINOSAUR
Brough Girling & Stephen Dell

KIT'S CASTLE
Chris Powling & Anthony Lewis

MISS WIRE AND THE THREE KIND MICE
Ian Whybrow & Emma Chichester Clark

MR COOL
Jacqueline Wilson & Stephen Lewis

PRINCESS ROSA'S WINTER
Judy Hindley & Margaret Chamberlain

WATCH OUT, WILLIAM
Kady MacDonald Denton